P9-DDX-751

Goldie Blox

GOLDIE BLOX AND THE BEST FRIEND FAIL!

To Stacey and Jess—my "sisters" and friends
—S.M.

 Published in the United States by Random House Children's Books, a division of Penguin Random House LLC, 1745 Broadway, New York, NY 10019, and in Canada by Penguin Random House Canada Limited, Toronto. Random House and the colophon are registered trademarks of Penguin Random House LLC. GoldieBlox and all related titles, logos, and characters are trademarks of GoldieBlox, Inc.

Visit us on the Web!
rhcbooks.com
GoldieBlox.com

Library of Congress Cataloging-in-Publication Data
Names: McAnulty, Stacy, author. | Marlin, Lissy, illustrator.
Title: Goldie Blox and the best friend fail / written by Stacy McAnulty ; illustrated by Lissy Marlin.
Other titles: Best friend fail
Description: New York : Random House, [2018] | Series: Goldie Blox and the Gearheads ; 4
Identifiers: LCCN 2017031178 (print) | LCCN 2017043284 (ebook)
ISBN 978-1-5247-6805-8 (trade) |
ISBN 978-1-5247-6806-5 (lib. bdg.) ISBN 978-1-5247-6807-2 (ebook)
Subjects: | BISAC: JUVENILE FICTION / Media Tie-In.
JUVENILE FICTION / Humorous Stories.
JUVENILE FICTION / Science & Technology.
Classification: LCC PZ7.M47825255 (ebook) |
LCC PZ7.M47825255 Gms 2018 (print) | DDC [Fic]—dc23

Printed in the United States of America
10 9 8 7 6 5 4 3 2 1

GOLDIE BLOX AND THE BEST FRIEND FAIL!

Written by Stacy McAnulty
Illustrated by Lissy Marlin

Random House New York

HONEY HAM AND JALAPEÑO WAFFLES

"Attention! Attention!" Goldie Blox banged her hammer on the desk in the front of the classroom. She didn't have a judge's gavel, but she always carried her tools.

"Thank you all for coming," she said to her eight classmates. "I call the first meeting of the Future Astronauts Club to order."

Higgs Bozon Prep (or HiBo, as everyone called it) had hundreds of after-school clubs, but none of them had ever involved space exploration. Until now.

Goldie's best friends Li "Gravity" Zhang and Val Voltz sat in the front row. Her other BFF, Ruby Rails, wasn't there because she was at CCC (Cool Coders Club).

"The mission of HiBo's Future Astronauts Club is to land on Mars by spring break," Goldie announced.

"That's not much into the future," Val mumbled.

"Can we also go to Venus?" asked a boy in the second row.

"Absolutely," answered Goldie.

"And Jupiter?" asked a girl holding a telescope.

Goldie nodded. "Adding it to our list. But first, we will send a mini-rocket into orbit and have snacks."

The mini-launch was a success. The model rocket—with nine tiny dolls to represent the club members—sailed into the blue sky. Then the kids enjoyed granola bars dipped in chocolate and hot sauce. Before the meeting came to a close, they elected officers for their new club. Goldie became president, Li was voted vice president, and Val took on the role of secretary. The girl with the telescope wanted to be treasurer.

"Should we have our next meeting Friday or Saturday?" Val asked.

"Either is fine with me," Goldie said.

"Saturday it is." Val wrote it down.

Later that afternoon, Goldie rode her skateboard to Bloxtown Park for the annual recycled-materials tower-building event. She loved making inventions with junk other people threw out. Goldie had started the event in Bloxtown three years ago. Not only was it super fun, it also raised money for charity. People donated money to Bloxtown's Summer Camp for each twenty-foot-tall tower the teams built. The first year, there had only been five. This year, it looked like they'd complete thirty-one towers.

With her basset hound, Nacho, at her side, Goldie got to work. They made a foundation of old tires. Then they added a layer of wooden pallets and paint cans. Nacho fetched, and Goldie built. She pulled a tape measure from her hair. Her wild and crazy blond curls acted like an extra pocket for all her stuff. Their tower was eleven feet high when it began to rain. They needed nine more feet.

Everyone ran beneath the picnic shelter.

"Sorry, folks," the organizer said. "You'll have to finish these on Saturday. I hope everyone comes back. Remember, this is for a good cause. You're sending kids to camp."

Goldie waved goodbye and jumped on her skateboard. She didn't mind the rain. Neither did Nacho. As they raced home, they hit every puddle.

They were soaked by the time they arrived at the BloxShop. Technically, it was a garage, but Goldie had transformed it into her workshop years earlier.

"This is the perfect time to try my Quick-Dry Blower," Goldie said. They stood in front of her invention. "Here goes nothing." Goldie flicked it on. It was a windstorm of warm air. The windows rattled, and boxes flew across the room. But she and Nacho were dry in seconds.

Goldie's parents, Junie and Beau Blox, came running in.

"What was that?" her mom asked. "Sounded like a tornado."

"It kinda was!" Goldie laughed. "The wind from my new invention was strong. I'm surprised it didn't blow the freckles off my arms." She looked at her arms. She still had freckles.

"Goldie, we have some

good news," her dad said.

Goldie bounced up and down. She loved good news. It was her favorite kind of news.

"You've won the waffle recipe contest!" he said.

"And the TV station wants to interview you and try your honey ham and jalapeño waffles," her mom added. "They'll be here on Saturday."

Goldie pumped her fist in the air. She'd never won a cooking contest before.

"That's awesome!" Goldie cried. Her parents each gave her a high five and a hug. "I can't wait to tell the Gearheads." The Gearheads were what Goldie called Ruby, Li, and Val.

She invited them over to celebrate. Li lived next door and arrived first. Val and Ruby came over a bit later. Goldie made popcorn and smoothies. Celebrating with friends made any victory sweeter.

"Cheers!" They raised their smoothies. "To Goldie."

"Thanks, Gearheads. I couldn't have done it without you." They had taste-tested seventeen different waffles before Goldie had finally come up with the winning recipe.

"I've got some news, too," Ruby said, smiling.

"What, Rubes?" Goldie asked.

"I've been asked to present at HackerCon," Ruby said. "It's been a dream of mine since I started coding. I went to my first convention when I was three."

"What's HackerCon?" Val asked. "Sounds like a place for people that have bad colds." She made a coughing sound.

"No, Val. It's a festival for the best computer coders and hackers. I can't believe I'll be talking to hundreds of people about my latest

app." Ruby pulled out her minicomputer to demonstrate. She took a photo of Goldie, then aimed the camera at Nacho. Next, she used her app to mash Goldie's and Nacho's pictures together.

"That's so cool," Goldie said.

"Way to go, Ruby!" Li added.

"Isn't hacking illegal?" Val asked.

Ruby laughed. "The criminal hackers don't usually go to conventions. We're all legit."

They raised their smoothies again, this time to Ruby.

"Thanks," Ruby said. "And, Goldie, I was hoping you'd be my co-presenter. You were the one who inspired me. Well, you and Nacho. I'll need help demonstrating my app and running the slideshow. I can't do it alone."

"Aww, Rubes. Of course! Nacho and I would be happy to help." Goldie wrapped an arm around Ruby's shoulder.

"Great," Ruby said. "HackerCon is this Saturday."

SOME QUICK QUANTUM PHYSICS BEFORE SCHOOL

Goldie crawled across the monkey bars, swung from the ceiling fan, bounced off the trampoline, and thumped down onto her bed.

"A perfect landing!"

Nacho curled up next to her. Goldie was exhausted. She closed her eyes and imagined new inventions she would engineer the next day. But she couldn't fall asleep. Something was tickling her brain.

Goldie tossed and turned for an hour.

"What am I forgetting?" she whispered to Nacho. He didn't have the answer.

Finally, her eyelids grew heavy, and closed. She was almost asleep, when . . .

"SATURDAY!" She shot up in bed. She had agreed to do everything on Saturday. She was happy that she'd remembered but worried that she wouldn't get to do it all.

Goldie threw back the covers and jumped out of bed. She slid down the fireman's pole to the kitchen.

"What are you doing up so late?" her mom asked.

"What time is the TV interview on Saturday?" she asked.

"The reporter will be here to try your waffles and talk about your winning recipe at one p.m.," her dad said with a smile. He'd taught her everything he knew about cooking.

Goldie went back upstairs and rode the zip line to Li's house. She tapped on his window.

"What's up, G?" he asked, yawning.

"When is our Future Astronauts Club meeting?"

"One o'clock on Saturday," he answered. "You'll be there, right? You are the prez. Our members are counting on you."

Goldie felt a small knot in her stomach.

"Yeah. Of course! Bye." She ran to the BloxShop. On her computer, she looked at the website for the recycled-materials tower-building event.

Rescheduled for one o'clock on Saturday.

"Oh no," Goldie mumbled. The knot in her stomach grew bigger and tighter, like she had swallowed a nest of bungee cords.

She called Ruby.

"Hey, Rubes, any chance HackerCon is *not* at one p.m. on Saturday?" Goldie crossed her fingers.

"It goes all day, but we present at one-thirty."

Phew! Goldie thought.

"But we need to be there at one to set up. Maybe even earlier. I'd hate to be late," Ruby said.

"I'll try," Goldie said.

"You'll be there, right?" Ruby asked. "I need you, Goldie. I can't do this alone."

"I promise." Goldie hung up the phone and took a deep breath. She had four things at the exact same time. A challenge for sure, but she loved a challenge. "I can engineer that," she said to herself.

The next morning, Goldie invited Li over early to help with a solution. On her whiteboard, she'd drawn out the problem.

One Goldie.

One time.

Four places.

"Looks like you'll need to choose, G," Li said. "What's most important?"

"They're all important. So that's why we need to invent a time machine."

"Awesome," he said. "I'm in."

They dragged in an old washing machine from the scrap pile behind the house. The Gearheads believed that everything could be reused. And it could have a new purpose. Goldie took the motherboard from her computer. Li borrowed parts from a lawn mower.

"Most physicists don't think time travel is possible," Li pointed out as they welded pieces together.

"I'm not trying to travel to dinosaur times," Goldie said. "I just need to *pause* time so I can do all four things at once."

"Got it." Li smiled. "We're using quantum physics, then."

"Well, technically, we're using a washing machine." They finished their invention and had just enough time to try it out before school.

"Hurry! We're going to be late," Li said.

"Not if our invention works." Goldie entered the data into the computer. She dropped an old action figure into the washing machine.

"It should spin fast enough that the doll will be in the BloxShop at the same time as she's outside in the front yard."

"Right," Li said. "To us it'll look like the exact same time, but to the doll it'll be one minute in the yard and one minute in the shop. Time is relative."

Goldie smiled. "I'm glad you're a physics genius. Let's fire this up!" She pressed the ON button and started the motor. The machine whirled and whined. A bit of smoke drifted from beneath it.

“It’s working!” Li shouted as the machine spun. And spun. All the forces lifted it an inch off the ground. Li and Goldie backed up. Nacho whimpered and ran inside the house.

“We’re going to put a hole in time!” Goldie yelled over the noise.

Suddenly, the washing machine shot across the room. It slammed through the wall, then fell on its side and finally went silent.

“Maybe not a hole in time, but we did put one in the wall,” Li said.

Goldie’s parents rushed into the BloxShop. Goldie explained their experiment and what had gone wrong.

“Maybe you should do more research before playing with quantum physics,” her dad said.

Goldie nodded reluctantly. "You're right."

"Come on, kids. I'll give you a ride to school," her mom said. She taught biology at HiBo and knew lots about plants but little about time travel.

All day during class, Goldie brainstormed other ways to be at her four activities at the same time. She finally figured out that the solution would require jetpacks and holograms. And maybe being a little late.

After the last bell rang, Ruby stopped Goldie in the hall. "Look!" She pulled out two matching jackets. CREATIVE BRAINS STUNNING APPS was sewn onto the back. "They're waterproof, have a tracking device, and will never stain. Plus, gray and aqua are this season's colors."

"These are so cool," Goldie said.

"We can wear them to HackerCon," Ruby

explained. “I think we’ll make a bigger impact if we match. Okay?”

“Absolutely.”

“Thanks, Goldie. You’re the best.” Ruby gave her a hug.

I hope *I’m the best*, Goldie thought. She’d need to be if she was going to pull this off.

HACKERCON, HERE WE COME

On Saturday, Goldie got up early and went to work. She had borrowed a hologram machine from the labs at HiBo. She needed it to project herself as a 3-D image for the Future Astronauts Club meeting. Goldie had to promise eighteen times not to rewire or make adjustments to the machine, and she kept her word. But she did make adjustments to her skateboard.

"Until I can teleport," she said to Nacho, "a jetpack on my skateboard will have to

do." She added a sidecar Nacho, with an airbag and parachute for safety.

Goldie had a plan that didn't involve time travel, but it allowed her to do everything she wanted. She would handle the waffle interview and the Future Astronauts Club at the same time using the hologram machine. She figured that would only take five minutes. She could talk fast. Then she'd blast off to the recycled-materials tower-building event. With Nacho's help, she'd only need two or three minutes to finish. Then she'd go to HackerCon. She estimated she would get to Ruby about one-fifteen. Maybe one-twenty. That didn't leave a lot of time to set up, but she would be there to present.

The final bit of preparation was calling

Ruby to warn her that she would be a little late. "Hey, Rubes. I just wanted to let you know—"

"Hi, Goldie," Ruby interrupted. "I'm so excited about our presentation. I think it went really well when we practiced yesterday."

"It was great. But you should know, I might not be there exactly at one p.m."

"What?"

"I might be fifteen—um, five or, um . . . a few minutes late."

"Goldie, I need you there." Ruby's voice shook.

"I'll be there, Rubes," Goldie promised. This was all going to work. She just knew it.

At twelve-thirty, Goldie sat ready and waiting in the kitchen. She had the hologram recorder focused on herself. And Li had set up the projector at the meeting.

"Is it working?" Goldie asked. She danced around.

"We see you and your awesome moves," Li said through a microphone in the machine. Goldie could not see him or any of the other young astronauts, but she could hear them.

Goldie stopped dancing and whipped up a batch of her award-winning waffles. She had two dozen stacked on a plate when the doorbell rang.

The clock said five minutes before one p.m. She was already ahead of schedule!

Her dad brought the reporter to the kitchen. Goldie recognized her from TV. The woman was tall with white hair. A cameraman followed behind her.

"Nice to meet you, Angela Rodgers from Channel Four Eyewitness News," Goldie said, shaking the reporter's hand.

"And nice to meet you, Goldie Blox," Angela Rodgers said with a smile.

Goldie rushed Angela Rodgers to the kitchen table. She pulled out her chair. She placed a huge stack of waffles in front of her.

"Here are my award-winning waffles," Goldie said. "They're made with honey ham and jalapeño. I'm very proud to have won this contest. It's an honor. I want to thank all my fans. And a special thanks to my mom and dad."

Goldie looked into the camera and smiled and waved. Then she turned back to Angela Rodgers. "Are we good? Is that a wrap?"

Angela Rodgers's mouth hung open. "I didn't even ask a question yet."

Suddenly, Li's voice came through on the hologram machine. "I call the second meeting of the Future Astronauts Club to order," he said. "We'll start by taking attendance."

"I'm here. I'm here!" Goldie raised her right arm and bounced up and down.

"What's going on?" Angela Rodgers asked.

"Nothing," Goldie said. "Quick. Ask me your questions. And try the waffles." The kitchen clock already said it was two minutes after one.

"Who inspired you to cook?" Angela Rodgers asked.

At the same time, Li asked, "Who should be the first to orbit Mars?"

"My dad," Goldie said, answering Angela Rodgers's question.

"Your *dad*?" Li asked. "He wants to orbit Mars?"

"No, I wasn't talking to—"

"What's your secret ingredient?" Angela Rodgers asked. She took a bite of the waffles.

But Val asked a question, too. "What fuel do we need to get to Mars?"

"Jet fuel," Goldie said.

Angela Rodgers spit out her mouthful of waffles. "Disgusting!"

The cameraman was catching every minute of this disaster.

"Uggghhh," Goldie moaned.

Goldie's mom stepped forward from the doorway. "I don't think your plan is working, Goldie. Everyone is getting confused."

Goldie looked at Angela Rodgers. "My secret ingredient is ginger. My dad inspired me to be creative in the kitchen." Then she turned to the hologram machine. "We should all go to Mars together. And we'll need jet fuel. A lot of jet fuel."

Her watch buzzed. It was five minutes after one. Time to go.

"Thanks for a great interview." She shook Angela Rodgers's hand again. Then she saluted the hologram recorder. "Meeting adjourned."

"But wait, we didn't—" Li said.

"I wasn't—" Angela Rodgers said.

"So sorry," Goldie said, and raced out the door. She had placed her souped-up skateboard on the front steps. Nacho was waiting in his sidecar. They strapped on helmets and off they went.

When Goldie and Nacho arrived at the park, Goldie's heart sank. All the other builders were nearly done with their twenty-foot towers. Goldie and Nacho had nine feet to go. She took a deep breath.

"Come on, Nacho!"

Nacho fetched recycled materials from a pile. Goldie started throwing them on top of their structure.

"I could really use some rope to secure this," Goldie said. But she was in a hurry. She heaved boxes on top of planters on top of plastic milk jugs on top of wooden crates.

In no time, Goldie's tower was tall enough. And in no time, it began to sway.

"Watch out!" a man yelled. He was building right next to Goldie.

"That's not stable," someone else said.

Goldie's watch beeped again.

"We gotta go!" she said to Nacho. But they couldn't just leave their tower wobbling. It needed to be fixed. They would have to ride extra fast to HackerCon—like light-speed fast.

Goldie adjusted a few paint cans. Nacho found some old cords, and they secured them to the structure. Goldie used pieces from a broken swing set to brace the corners.

"Not perfect, but it works. Let's go."

As they ran to the skateboard, a strong wind blew. Goldie hoped her tower wouldn't fall down, but she didn't have time to check on it. She got on her board, and Nacho jumped into his sidecar.

She kicked her skateboard into the highest gear. She hoped to be with Ruby in three minutes.

Goldie and Nacho flew down the sidewalk. Goldie grabbed a street sign and took a hard right. They jumped over potholes and sailed through obstacles. Things were looking good until a cat ran out in front of them.

Nacho barked.

Goldie used her foot to brake.

They stopped and somehow managed not to hit the cat. But a wheel on her skateboard popped off.

"Oh no." Goldie looked at her watch. She'd

thought she'd be at the convention center by now.

"Come on, Nacho. We have to run."

Running was not Nacho's favorite activity. When he had to move, he walked slowly or used a jetpack.

Goldie sprinted up River Street and down Clark Road. Nacho tried to keep up. His tongue dragged on the sidewalk.

"Poor dog." Goldie picked him up and kept running, but just a little slower. She was out of breath and had a blister on her foot when she finally reached HackerCon.

It was one-forty-three p.m.

Goldie dashed up the stairs to the front door of the convention center. She had her palm on the handle when she heard crying. And, unfortunately, she recognized it.

Nacho and Goldie walked around the

building. They found Ruby sitting on the ground. Her legs were pulled to her chest, and her head rested on her knees. Ruby's minicomputer lay next to her. It was turned off.

Goldie sank to the ground. "Ruby."

Ruby lifted her head. She wiped her tears.

"I'm sorry I'm late." Goldie put a hand on Ruby's shoulder. "But I'm here now. Let's go present!" She forced a smile. She had a feeling

she knew what was coming next.

"We can't. We missed our shot." Ruby's shoulders shook.

"Maybe I can explain to the organizers." Goldie was back on her feet. "See, I had an interview and a meeting. There was a tower-building event. And then my skateboard broke down. I had to carry my dog three blocks, and he's not—"

"No, Goldie," Ruby interrupted. "You can't explain to anyone. You weren't here like you promised. It's over. It's done."

"I'm sorry. I should have been here." A knot formed again in her stomach.

Ruby nodded.

"Are you mad at me?" Goldie asked.

"Not mad," Ruby said. "Just . . ." She stopped talking.

Goldie had failed her best friend. She felt

awful. But she put on a big phony smile to cover it. "Hey, why don't we have a sleepover? We can start planning for next year's HackerCon. We'll do something great!"

"No thanks." Ruby stood and gathered her minicomputer and bag. "I want to be alone. Bye, Goldie."

Ruby walked away without looking back.

A RUBY-SHAPED BLIMP

Goldie invited Li and Val over to the BloxShop. She had disappointed Ruby and needed to fix the situation.

"I can't believe I missed HackerCon," Goldie said. She flopped down on the couch. Nacho licked her cheek. It didn't make her feel any better.

"Seriously?" Val asked. "You had to know you couldn't be in four places at once."

"I tried," Goldie said.

"Yeah, you did." Li pointed to the hole in

the wall from their time machine.

"We should patch that." Goldie got up and pulled out her hammer. Nacho dragged over some scrap wood, and Val picked up a can of nails. They got to work.

"Do you think Ruby will ever talk to me again?" Goldie asked as she hammered.

"Definitely," Li said.

"Of course," Val agreed. "Maybe you could make it up to her somehow."

Goldie sighed and kicked the now-broken washing machine. "If only my time machine worked. I'd go back and make it right. Should we try again?"

"Goldie." Val grabbed her by the shoulders. "Just write her a note. Say you're sorry and that it won't happen again. It's that simple."

"A note is a good idea, Val." Goldie ran over to her whiteboard. "A note written in the sky."

Val slapped her forehead. “I meant a note on paper.”

“We’re going to think of something great. Come on, Gearheads.” Saying *Gearheads* but not having Ruby there made Goldie’s stomach hurt. Their group was incomplete.

“You okay?” Li asked.

“I will be,” Goldie said. She turned to the whiteboard and wrote *skywriting*. They brainstormed other big ideas, like performing a rap song in Ruby’s honor during a school assembly.

“That doesn’t sound embarrassing at all,” Val said, rolling her eyes. “But I’d love a chance to write a new song.” Val was the musical one of the group.

They also added *parade* and *a Ruby-shaped blimp* to the list.

“Can you get a blimp made to look like a

person?" Val asked.

"We could engineer it," Goldie said. All these ideas were making her feel better.

"Hey, I just remembered something." Li jumped up as Goldie was writing *carve Ruby's face into Mount Rushmore.*

"What?" Val asked.

"Isn't Ruby's birthday next week?" Li said.

"You're right!" Goldie couldn't believe she had almost forgotten.

"We could have a party," Val suggested. "I can make a cake."

"No," Goldie said. "Not a party. A bash! A huge, surprise bash." Goldie erased all the other ideas from the board and wrote *BASH!!!*

"Ruby doesn't love surprises," Val pointed out. "Remember when you jumped out of her

BASH!!!

locker dressed as a polar bear? She almost fainted."

Goldie had only been trying to celebrate Earth Day in the most epic way.

"Yeah, G," Li agreed. "Ruby likes to plan and have everything in its place. She puts her socks in alphabetical order."

"Huh?" Goldie didn't understand.

"*B* for black socks comes before *D* for diagonally striped socks," Val explained. "She showed me her system one afternoon."

"Well, she's going to love this surprise bash." Goldie was certain. "Because we'll plan everything perfectly. We'll have it at Frothy Formulas Smoothie Shop, but it'll be fancy."

"I can do the decorations," Li volunteered. "It's for Ruby. So something high-tech. Laser lights, hidden speakers, disco balls, and large HD screens with Ruby's picture."

"Perfect!" Goldie declared.

"Over-the-top," Val mumbled.

"What about food?" Goldie asked. "Val, you're making the cake, right?"

"Yes, but it'll just be a cake. Don't expect it to fly or light up."

"Great, as long as it's yummy. But maybe the candles could shoot—"

"No!" Val interrupted. "The candles will just be candles. I'm not going to risk you sending my cake to the moon or blowing it up."

"Fine," Goldie agreed. "Now we need a guest list. We need to invite her favorite people."

"Like the girls on the cheerleading team and in her Cool Coders Club?" Val asked.

"Of course, but also her *favorite*, favorite people," Goldie said with a big smile.

"Who?" Li asked.

"Sarah Kumar and Zada!" Goldie had heard Ruby talk about these two women many times. They were her idols. Sarah Kumar was the world's most sought-after computer programmer, and Zada was an iconic fashion designer.

"Ruby would love to meet them," Val said. "But do you really think they'll come?"

"Yes." Goldie couldn't imagine why not.

"This is going to be epic," Li said.

"Now I just need to think of the perfect gift, and this will be the best birthday Ruby has ever had!" Goldie couldn't wait.

MEET ME BY BLOCK HEAD

Students filled the halls of Higgs Bozon Prep. The first bell had not rung yet. Goldie and Li walked past the aluminum cube statue that was HiBo's mascot.

"Morning, Block Head," Goldie said. She'd made up the nickname for the cube. She knew the reason behind the mascot: *Because like a student, an aluminum cube is full of potential.* Still, Goldie thought a tiger or a wrench would be a better choice. She hoped to convince the school to make a change. Someday. But right now, she had different mission.

"There she is." Goldie grabbed Li's arm and dragged him toward Val.

"Hey, guys," Val said as she put some books in her locker.

"We have a problem," Goldie said.

"What?" Val's eyes grew wide, and she started chewing on her nails. "Do I need to put on safety goggles?"

"No. Well, maybe." Goldie scratched her head. "I sent invitations to the special guests for the you-know-what." She looked around in case Ruby was nearby.

"And?" Val said.

"They haven't replied! If Sarah Kumar and Zada aren't there, this will be a disaster." Goldie wouldn't let Ruby's surprise birthday bash be a disaster.

"G, when did you send the invitations?" Li asked.

"Last night!"

"Maybe they haven't even seen it yet," Val pointed out. "Maybe we should wait a whole day before panicking."

"No. I'm not taking any chances. After school, I'm going to drop by Sarah Kumar's office and deliver another invitation." Goldie pulled an envelope from her hair. "Who's with me?"

"By 'drop by,' do you mean parachute into?" Val asked.

"No," Goldie shook her head. "Well, maybe."

"I'm in," Li said.

"Val?" Goldie asked.

"I guess," she answered. "But no parachutes for me."

"Awesome. Meet me by Block Head after

school." Goldie smiled. She knew that when her friends worked together, they could do anything.

Goldie was about to head to class when someone tapped her on the shoulder. She spun around. It was Ruby.

"Hi, Goldie," Ruby said.

"Hey," Goldie said nervously. She hoped Ruby hadn't overheard her plans.

"Um, I missed you this weekend," Ruby continued. "Can we put this whole HackerCon thing behind us? I know you didn't miss it on purpose. And—"

"I didn't miss it on purpose. And I'm so, so sorry. It'll never happen again." Goldie crossed her heart with her finger.

Ruby smiled. "Let's just not talk about it anymore."

"I missed you, too." Goldie hugged Ruby.

“Cool. The gang’s all back together,” Li said happily.

“So, do you Gearheads want to come watch me cheer after school today?” Ruby asked. “We’ve been working on a new halftime routine. Goldie, we’re using the magnetic shoes you invented to create a record-breaking pyramid.”

“That’s awesome! I’ll be there.” Goldie high-fived Ruby.

“Goldie . . . ,” Val mumbled. “Remember?”

“Right. Sorry. We can’t.” Goldie shrugged.

“What are you guys up to?” Ruby asked. She couldn’t keep the disappointment from her face.

“Nothing. Nothing,” Goldie said as the first bell rang. “Good luck with cheerleading.” They all headed into their classrooms.

After school, Li and Val waited by the aluminum cube. Goldie joined them, carrying what appeared to be a mini-helicopter.

"What's that?" Val asked. "You don't expect us to fly in it, do you?"

Goldie thought for a second. Then shook her head. "It can't hold us. This is to send a message to Ruby." She unrolled a banner that read GOOD LUCK, RUBY!! CHEER! CHEER! CHEER!

"I want Ruby to know we're thinking about

her." Goldie tied the banner to her Do-It-All drone and set it off toward the school's gym. The drone could drop confetti, play music, fly a banner, and take pictures. Goldie had painted it blue like the sky and white like clouds. She thought of it as camouflage for when she used it outside.

"Let's go!" Li said. "We have invitations to deliver."

Sarah Kumar had an office in the center of town. She had moved her company, Bit & Byte, to Bloxtown from Portland two years earlier. But Goldie had never met her. More importantly, Ruby had never met her, and Ruby idolized her.

Goldie knew a lot about Sarah Kumar, thanks to the report Ruby had done in school last month. Sarah wrote her first code when she was eight. (Ruby wrote her first at five.)

Sarah had hacked into the computers at the Coaster Town amusement park when she was in middle school. She'd set the ticket prices to ninety-nine cents for one day.

At first, the owners of Coaster Town were mad and wanted Sarah to be punished. But the day was a big success. And now they lowered their twenty-dollar ticket prices to ninety-nine cents one day every year for students. They actually called it Sarah Kumar Day.

Sarah had won every coding contest there was. She'd created apps that she sold for millions of dollars. She'd even met the president. He had needed help with the security on his personal computer. Sarah was an expert on that, too.

Sarah Kumar was one of the best coders in the world. But Goldie thought Ruby was, too. They needed to meet.

Val rode her bike, while Goldie and Li rode their boards. They kept their speed reasonable and obeyed all the traffic laws. Val preferred it that way. When they arrived at the high-rise building, they parked and went in the front door.

"This might be easy," Val said.

But she spoke too soon. The security guard at the desk wouldn't let them go to the thirteenth floor to meet Sarah Kumar.

"You need an appointment," he said.

"How do we get an appointment?" Val asked.

"Call her assistant." The guard pulled out a phone, pressed a few numbers, and handed it to Goldie.

"Sarah Kumar's office," a man answered on the other end.

"Hi, I'd like to make an appointment. Do you

have something available in, say, two minutes? This is very important," Goldie explained. Then she added, "Please."

"Ms. Kumar doesn't have any openings until April."

"April? That's two months away!" Goldie couldn't wait that long.

"No, sorry for the confusion. I meant next April. In fourteen months."

Goldie said no thanks and hung up the phone.

"Sorry, G," Li said as they headed to the door.

"I'm not giving up!" Goldie declared. "There are other ways to see Sarah Kumar on the thirteenth floor."

"Wait!" Val grabbed Goldie's shoulder. "Before you suggest using suction cups to climb the outside of the building like a spider,

maybe we can just borrow this." Val ran over to a life-size cardboard cutout of Sarah Kumar holding a laptop.

Val smiled. "I don't usually think stealing is a good idea, but it's probably safer than what you're thinking. And we'll bring it back."

Goldie's face lit up. "That's a great idea, Val. I just happen to have suction cups in my backpack."

Val smacked herself on the forehead.

DOUBLE-TIME IT

Goldie dropped her backpack and pulled out the suction cups and straps. She'd been carrying them for a few months. She knew they'd come in handy eventually.

"Put two on each shoe and one in each palm." She handed the suction cups to Li and Val.

Val looked up at the building. It was twenty stories high—the tallest building in Bloxtown. "I can't do this. I'll stand here with a net and catch you when . . . I mean, *if* you fall."

"You're coming," Goldie told Val. "And no one is going to fall." She reached into her backpack again and took out rope and grappling hooks.

"See?" Li said. "Goldie always considers safety first."

"Well . . ." Goldie scratched her chin. "Maybe not first, but usually second or third. On occasion, fourth."

Li tied the ropes to the hooks, and Goldie used the launcher to send them to the roof. She tugged the three ropes. They were secure.

"We're ready," she announced.

Li went first. He climbed up the side of the building to the thirteenth floor in record time. "Come on!" he shouted to Goldie and Val.

"You go next," Goldie said to Val. "And open

your eyes. It'll be easier."

Val trembled with every move. Goldie stayed right behind her.

"Good job, Val."

Val slowly crawled up the building. They were halfway to the thirteenth floor when Val's foot slipped. The rope kept her safe. But she screamed and dropped her headphones.

"Oh . . . uh," Goldie said.

"It's okay. I'm sure you can fix them," Val said as they looked down at her busted headphones.

"Not that." Goldie put a finger to her mouth. The security guard had come outside.

Li snuck into a vent. Val and Goldie smushed against the building like bugs on a windshield. Goldie hoped no one would see them.

"It'll be okay," Goldie assured Val.

They stayed perfectly still as the security guard walked around below. They were so still, Goldie wasn't sure Val was breathing. He seemed to be taking forever. Goldie wished Ruby was with them. Using her minicomputer, she could make the phone inside ring or something.

Finally, they heard the door open and close. Goldie snuck a peek. The guard was gone.

“Coast is clear!” Li yelled down. “Double-time it!”

“You heard Sergeant Li Gravity.” Goldie patted Val’s back. “Get moving.”

Val climbed a little faster. But not exactly double time.

“This way,” Li said. “In the vent.” He led them through the tight hole. They had to slide on their bellies to fit.

Li went straight, then left, then right, and then another right. He looked through the vents, trying to find Sarah Kumar’s office. Finally, he stopped at a grate that blocked the end of the vent.

“I see her!” he whispered over his shoulder. “She’s at her desk.”

Goldie handed him a screwdriver she was carrying in her hair. He quietly removed the grate. Then, not so quietly, they slithered like snakes into her office.

Goldie, Li, and Val were Gearheads, not ninjas. They landed in a tangled pile and took a minute to free themselves. Li and Goldie jumped to their feet. But Val kissed the tile floor.

"I'll never leave you again," she muttered to the ground.

"Who are you?" Sarah asked. She stood behind her desk. Goldie had expected her to look like the cardboard cutout in the lobby. Maybe wearing a suit or other work clothes, with smooth, silky hair. This Sarah wore a hoodie and sweatpants, and her black hair was in a sloppy ponytail.

"Hello, Ms. Kumar," Goldie said with a smile. "We are the Gearheads." Then, for some reason, she bowed.

"Okay. Are you dangerous? Should I call

security?" Sarah used a pencil to scratch her head. "Wait, are you here to sell popcorn and cookies? Because I'll buy ten cases of every flavor, but you can't tell my doctor. I promised her I'd give up salt, sugar, and coffee. I also promised I'd try to sleep at least an hour every night."

"Sorry, we're out of snacks." Li pulled out the lining of his empty pockets.

"We're here with an invitation," Goldie explained.

"That's very kind," Sarah said. She sank back into her chair, and her fingers started working her laptop. "But I'm extremely busy. You can just mail me my award." She waved her hand toward a wall behind the Gearheads.

Goldie turned. She'd never seen so many trophies, medals, certificates, and plaques. HiBo had hundreds, maybe even a thousand.

Sarah Kumar had more.

Val finally stood up. She wasn't shaking anymore. "No awards. We're inviting you to a friend's birthday party."

"Bash! Birthday *bash*!" Goldie corrected her.

"I don't attend kids' birthday parties or bashes. I don't like clowns and piñatas." Sarah shuddered.

Goldie started laughing.

"What?" Sarah asked.

"Like Ruby Rails would ever want a clown at her party." Goldie kept laughing. Val and Li joined in.

"Did you say 'Ruby Rails'?" Sarah stood up again. "*The* Ruby Rails?"

Goldie nodded. "The one and only."

"I've wanted to meet Ruby for a long time," Sarah said. "I was hoping to meet her at

HackerCon, but her presentation was canceled at the last minute."

Goldie's stomach tightened. That was her fault. She forced herself to smile and take a deep breath.

"Well, here's your chance." Goldie handed Sarah an invitation.

"Thank you," said Sarah. She tucked the invitation into her pocket. "I'll be there."

Goldie pumped her fist in the air. Li danced in victory. But Val didn't look happy.

"What's wrong?" Goldie asked her.

"Can we take the elevator down? Or are we using the suction cups again?" Val chewed her lower lip.

"We could flip a coin," Li suggested.

Val turned green.

"I think we should take the elevator," Goldie said.

A GB ORIGINAL DESIGN

Goldie, Val, and Li sat around the BloxShop with Goldie's laptop open. Their excitement about meeting Sarah Kumar—and giving her the invitation—was fading. Because now they needed to find Zada, one of the world's greatest fashion designers.

Val read from a biography website. "Her closest offices are in New York and LA. But she was born in Bloxtown. That's an interesting fact."

"That's probably one of the reasons Ruby loves her," Goldie pointed out. "Zada is a hometown girl."

"Sort of," Val said. "It says here she only lived in Bloxtown for eighteen months. She moved to Milan before she was two."

"Any chance she's coming home for a visit sometime soon?" Goldie asked, flopping back onto the couch.

"I'll check," Val said. She clicked the mouse.

Li tried to make Goldie feel better. "G, it's still awesome that you got Sarah Kumar. If we can't get Zada, that's okay."

"Hey!" Val exclaimed. "Guess what?"

"Zada is coming to town tomorrow to talk to fans at the mall?" Goldie guessed. That would make life easy for sure.

"Um, no." Val shook her head. "But she will be in Southwell on Saturday afternoon for a junior fashion show."

"Southwell?" Li asked. "That's only forty-five minutes away if we take the high-speed train."

"Awesome!" Goldie jumped up.

"Wait," Val said. "Goldie, you should double-check your schedule."

"Oh, my schedule is clear. I'll be there!" She laughed.

"But we need a plan for how to get Zada an invitation," Val said. "It could be crowded. She probably has security. And I'm not crawling up the side of another building."

"We could drop a thousand invitations from an airplane," Goldie suggested.

Li raised his hand. "I volunteer to fly the airplane or to jump out of it."

"That's not very environmentally friendly," Val said. "I may have found a better way. Look!"

Goldie and Li gathered around the computer. They read about the junior fashion show. Contestants could enter one outfit, and the winner would get his or her picture taken with Zada. If she really liked the outfit, she would add it to her spring line.

"Ruby should totally enter," Li said.

"She can't." Goldie pointed to the word *junior*. "Ruby has been designing and selling her fashions since she was in diapers."

"And even those diapers were fashionable," Val added. "I've seen the pictures. Denim, fake fur, jewels. All very cool."

"It's good that Ruby can't enter, because I need to win. When I do, I'll get my picture with

Zada. That's when I'll personally deliver her invitation!"

"All you have to do is design your own clothes," Val said.

"I can engineer that!" Goldie took out every marker she owned and started sketching in her graph-paper notebook. She drew buttons and straps. She added pockets. Li and Val watched quietly. Finally, Goldie held up her masterpiece.

"Nice." Li smiled.

"Um, it's nice," Val agreed. "But it kinda looks like the overalls you're wearing. Just with more colors."

"No," Goldie said. "I also changed the pocket shape from a rectangle to a square."

Li nodded. Val wrinkled her face.

"You're right. I'll keep working on it." Goldie turned the page on her first GB original design.

Li and Val went home for the night. Goldie was left to work with only Nacho. He didn't add much to the project, except when he shook. Then Goldie's designs were covered with brown-and-white fur.

She tried drawing fancy dresses, cargo shorts, frilly blouses, and boots with chunky heels. But none of it seemed like her style. So she went back to purple overalls.

"I wish Ruby was here," Goldie said to Nacho. "She'd know how to help me."

Nacho looked up. He seemed to miss Ruby, too.

"She'd tell me to try something new. But she'd also say to stay true to myself." Goldie sighed. "I miss Ruby. And not only because I need help designing clothes."

Nacho rested his head on Goldie's lap. She scratched behind his ears. They had to design this outfit without Ruby's help because they were doing it *for* Ruby. "Let's get back to work," she said.

Nacho licked her cheek.

Goldie sketched another pair of overalls. It was 100 percent Goldie. But she wanted to dress them up with Blox style. She added expandable wings so the overalls could turn into a flight suit. She held up her design.

"Not bad. Let's get sewing." She took an old pair of overalls from her room. She borrowed a sewing machine from her parents.

"What are you going to turn our sewing machine into?" her dad asked. "A pineapple slicer?"

"Maybe something retro, like a rotary telephone?" her mom asked.

"No, I just want to use it as a sewing machine," Goldie said. Her parents looked confused.

She carried it back to the BloxShop. Maybe she would re-engineer it into something when she was finished making the glide overalls.

It took her several tries to work the sewing machine. She was better at welding. And the first prototype had a giant wing on the left but a tiny wing on the right.

"Oops." She pulled out the stitches and fixed her mistakes.

After she finished the glide overalls, she

redesigned her sneakers. In the soles, she added a machine for special effects like fog and laser lights. She changed the outsides, too, painting them red and gold.

The final touch to Goldie's outfit was a new belt. She called it the Swiss Army Belt. It had a bungee cord, an antenna, and a spoon. Plus, it could open a can of beans.

Goldie laid out her design on the BloxShop

floor. Purple overalls, red-and-gold sneakers, and an orange belt. They were all functional and comfortable, but not exactly high fashion. She wanted to call Ruby and ask for advice, but she knew she couldn't.

Just then Nacho knocked over two cans of paint and walked through them.

"Uh-oh," Goldie said. She went to get towels to clean up after Nacho, but when she came back, he had walked across her outfit.

"What did you . . ." Goldie stopped mid-sentence. Her outfit actually looked better with colorful paw prints. She reached down and patted her dog. "Nice work, boy."

Next, Goldie coated her hands in glitter and added the sparkles to her clothes. "What do you think?" she asked Nacho.

But he didn't answer. He had fallen asleep.

Goldie studied her design. She liked it.

She thought she had a chance at winning. But something was still wrong. She swallowed the lump in her throat, because she knew what was missing.

Ruby.

PAW PRINTS WERE TWO SEASONS AGO

Everything was on schedule. Li, Val, and Goldie took the high-speed train to Southwell. They signed in for the junior fashion show. Goldie and Val stood backstage, waiting for her turn to strut the runway. She wore her newly designed outfit with pride.

"Where's Zada? Have you seen her?" Goldie held an invitation in each hand. She'd brought along an extra just in case.

"Don't worry," Val said, which was something she didn't get to say often. "She's in the audience. You'll get to meet her when you win."

And if I don't win? Goldie decided not to think about that possibility.

"Li's keeping an eye on her, too," Val continued. "If she tries to leave early or something, he'll let us know."

Someone clapped loudly three times.

"Junior designers, time to line up," a woman with a clipboard instructed.

"Good luck!" Val gave Goldie a hug. "I'm going to go watch. By the way, I think you look great."

Val left, and Goldie lined up behind a redheaded girl in a beautiful dress that hung to her knees. The gray-and-pink fabric reflected the backstage lights.

"I like your dress," Goldie told her.

"Thanks." The girl twirled, and the bottom

of the dress expanded.

"That's awesome. Have you thought of adding propellers to the hem?" Goldie asked. "You might be able to design the world's first hover dress. You could fly."

"Really? I never thought of that. Do you think that could work?" the girl asked.

Goldie shrugged. "It's worth a try. Even if the first prototype doesn't work, eventually you'll get it." That was the secret to Goldie's success. She believed every one of her designs would work eventually. They rarely did on the first or second try. But give her a hundred chances and a team like the Gearheads, and she could make anything work.

The contestants began walking through the curtain one at a time. Goldie had butterflies in her stomach. This was new to her.

"I like your look, too," the girl whispered.

Goldie nodded. "Thanks."

It was the girl's turn. She waved goodbye and walked through the curtain and onto the runway. Goldie took a breath, ready to go next. She switched the button on her sneakers to activate them.

The woman with a clipboard nodded to Goldie.

"Wait!" a voice yelled.

"Don't go out there!" shouted another voice.

Goldie turned to see Li and Val running toward her. They were waving their hands for her to stop.

The woman with the clipboard cleared her throat.

"Sorry. One second." Goldie stepped aside, and a boy in a blue-and-black sweat suit took her place. His outfit had cool racing stripes, and Goldie wondered for a second if they were aerodynamic. They certainly made him look fast.

Val and Li stopped in front of her.

"Ruby's here!" Li said.

"Right in the front row," Val added. "She's not a contestant, but she's watching." She pulled back the curtain. They could see Ruby sitting with her mom and little sister to the right of the runway.

"I can't go out there," Goldie said. "Ruby

will see me and ask why I'm here. That'll ruin the surprise." And she couldn't make up an excuse because there was none that wouldn't hurt Ruby's feelings. There was no good reason—other than the truth—for Goldie to enter a fashion show without telling Ruby about it.

"Maybe we could ask that lady to give an invitation to Zada for us." Li pointed to the woman with the clipboard. She gave Goldie an angry look. She was not happy that a contestant was holding up the show.

Goldie shook her head. "I need to hand deliver it to Zada and tell her why she must be at the party."

"What are you going to do?" Val asked.

Another junior designer walked onto the runway. There were only three left. The Gearheads were running out of time.

Goldie looked down at her outfit. It was fun, thanks to the paw prints and glitter. But it was also functional.

"I've got this," she said with a wink. Goldie went back in line for the runway and left Li and Val wondering.

"I guess we'll find out," Li said to Val. They went back into the audience.

Goldie was the last person in line.

"Are you ready this time?" the woman asked.

"Absolutely."

The woman opened the curtain, and Goldie tapped her heels together. Immediately, fog shot out of her sneakers. She turned so the gray mist would fill the right side of the room and keep Ruby from seeing her.

But the fog wasn't easy to control. It swept across the right side of the room. Then it filled

the rest of the auditorium.

Goldie turned on the laser lights in the toe of her sneakers. That just made it harder to see. Though it was completely safe, the crowd got up. People headed to the doors. Everyone was talking.

"Where's the exit?"

"What's going on?"

"Are we at a rock concert?"

Goldie couldn't see either, but she needed to find Zada. She couldn't miss her chance. She pulled the cord under her left arm. The wings on her overalls folded up. She slowly made her way to the end of the stage and jumped up. She soared above the scattering crowd.

It was still hard to see. Luckily, she had night vision glasses in her Swiss Army Belt. She popped them on and spotted Zada making her way out the back door.

Goldie turned and flew out right behind the iconic fashion designer. She came to a perfect landing in the parking lot.

Zada stared at Goldie. Her mouth hung open.

"Hi, I'm Goldie Blox." She pushed the glasses off her face. "Nice to meet you."

"What, my darling, are you wearing?" Zada asked.

"Glide overalls, a Swiss Army Belt, and special-effect sneakers." Goldie held out her arms and turned to show off her outfit.

"Your design might be a bit dated. Paw prints were two seasons ago. But I love your mix of fashion and function, darling. Bravo!" Zada clapped her hands quietly.

"If you like this, then you need to see my friend Ruby's designs," Goldie said. "She's a fashion genius. Probably the best fashion designer in the world!"

Zada smirked.

"Except for you, of course," Goldie said and shrugged. "Ruby has this skirt that's also a speaker. It's great if you ever want to have a sudden dance party."

"That's a fabulous idea. I'd love to see it."

"Well, you can." Goldie pulled an invitation out of her pocket. "We're having a birthday bash for Ruby. She's your biggest fan. She'd love to meet you."

Zada took the envelope and opened it. "Hmmm . . . I'm very busy. But I'll make it work. See you then, darling."

Goldie flew off and found Li and Val. "Mission accomplished."

THE WEATHER ON MARS

Val and Goldie went to Frothy Formulas. Val ordered a berry smoothie, and Goldie had the Blox Special. It was made with yogurt, mint, pineapple, bananas, and maple syrup. It was called the Blox Special because only Goldie and her dad ever requested it.

"I can't wait for the party," Miss Maggie, the owner, said. "Are you kids all set?"

"Val's got the food for the party covered," Goldie said.

"Yep. Cake. Traditional birthday party

food." Val raised her chin.

"I guess that'll work for a birthday bash, too," Goldie said.

"I'll supply the smoothies," Miss Maggie added. "It's my specialty."

Goldie nodded and took a big gulp. "And Li's got the decorations. We've invited all the guests. Now I just need the perfect gift."

"I'm sure you'll think of something." Miss Maggie smiled and went back to the cash register to help a customer.

"Do you have any ideas?" Val asked.

"Not yet. But it's going to be something big! Epic!" Goldie held her hands out wide.

"You only have two days," Val reminded her. "And you need . . ." She stopped talking and nodded toward the front door.

Goldie turned. Ruby and her family walked into Frothy Formulas.

"Quick. Get down!" Goldie sank under the table.

"Why are we hiding?" Val whispered.

"I don't want to ruin the surprise," Goldie said. *Or hurt Ruby's feelings because we didn't invite her out for smoothies*, she thought.

"She's not going to know what we were talking about," Val said.

Ruby stopped next to their table.

"Hi, Val. Hi, Goldie. What are you doing?"

Goldie crawled out from under the table. "I was just looking for something. And drinking a smoothie. And talking about the weather. The weather on Mars. Just talking with Val about that stuff and nothing else." She was nervous and couldn't stop talking.

Ruby gave her a puzzled look.

"What are *you* up to, Ruby?" Val asked.

"You're not going to believe what happened. I went to a fashion show in Southwell yesterday. Zada was there. She's my all-time favorite designer. She's a legend. She's my idol." Ruby pointed to the logo on her shirt, pants, and socks. All of them said Zada.

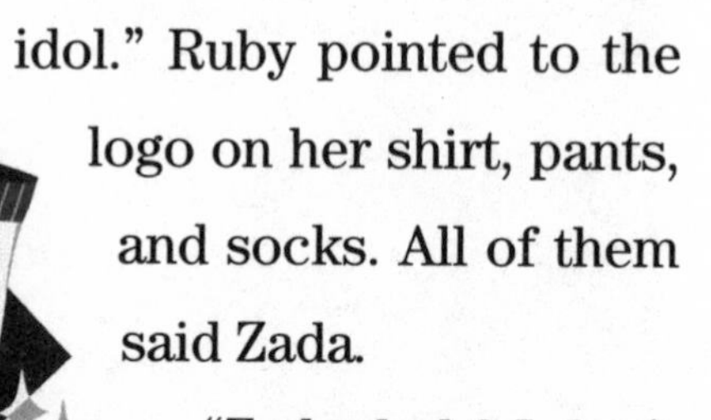

"Zada, huh? I don't even know who that

is." Goldie tried to play it cool, but she had a feeling she was doing a terrible job.

"I was hoping to meet her," Ruby continued. "My mom got us VIP tickets and everything. It was a junior fashion show, so I wasn't allowed to enter."

"Well, did you meet her?" Val asked.

"No." Ruby frowned. "The room suddenly filled with fog, and the rest of the show was canceled. I was so close to meeting her."

"I'm sorry," Goldie whispered.

Ruby shrugged. "It's not your fault."

Goldie slumped in her chair. She knew it actually was.

"Maybe you'll get to meet her some other time," Val said. "Maybe soon."

Goldie kicked Val under the table.

"Ow!" Val shouted.

"I'm going to order a smoothie," Ruby said.

"Then I'll join you. I feel like I've hardly seen you guys all week." She turned to go to the counter.

"Wait, Ruby," Goldie said. "Sorry, but we're about to leave." She needed to work on Ruby's present. And she didn't trust herself to keep the surprise birthday bash quiet.

Ruby blinked a bunch of times. Her mouth curved down. "Oh." She looked even more disappointed than when she'd talked about not meeting Zada.

"I can stay," Val said. "I'll hang out with you, Ruby."

"Thanks, Val." Ruby gave her a smile.

Goldie felt awful. "Okay, I'll see you guys later." And she left on her own.

Engineering new designs always made Goldie feel better. It kept her brain and her hands busy. With Nacho's help, she started working on a present for Ruby. Nacho fetched while Goldie welded, hammered, and tinkered. Her design slowly came together.

Li flew through an open window and into the BloxShop just as Goldie was finishing.

"I'm glad you're here, Li. I want to show you what I've made for Ruby."

Li took a seat on a stool and spun around. "Let's see it."

Goldie plugged in her invention. Then she called over Nacho to demonstrate. She offered him a waffle. A hug or a waffle were the only payment her dog ever needed.

"It's a hair dryer that also gives back massages," she explained. She dumped a cup of water on Nacho's head. Then she turned on her newest invention.

The hair dryer blew warm air across

Nacho's wet head. Mechanical arms projected from the sides. They massaged Nacho's back. The dog closed his eyes, and his tongue hung out of his mouth.

"Awesome!" Li said. "She'll love it."

But he spoke too soon. The hands moved from Nacho's back to his head. And instead of massaging, they started styling.

"Um . . ." Goldie twisted a knob. "It just needs some adjustments."

Nacho's eyes flew open. He tried to step away, but the arms held firm. He whimpered.

"G, maybe you should turn it off," Li suggested.

"I'm trying." Goldie flicked a switched. Pressed a button. And finally, pulled the plug.

"Wow!" Li said.

Goldie put the hair dryer down. Then she looked at Nacho. He had a spiky hairdo.

"I think it looks good," Goldie said.

Nacho trotted over to a mirror. When he first saw his reflection, he growled. But then he realized the dog in the mirror was him. He examined himself from the front, from the left, from the right. His doggy smile came back.

"He likes it!" Goldie laughed.

"Yeah," Li said. "But I can't imagine Ruby would like that hairstyle."

"No, not at all. I need to come up with something else. Will you help me?" she asked.

"Absolutely, G."

Goldie put the hair dryer away and showed Li her other idea. It wasn't working yet.

"I call it the Friend-a-Wear, or FaW." She held out two small devices and explained how they were supposed to work. "With FaW, Ruby will always know when I'm thinking about her."

"Totally cool, G. One of your best inventions yet. I love it," Li said. "And Ruby will love it, too."

"I know. But it's not working." She snapped one on her wrist and pressed the button. Nothing happened. "See. Something's not right. It's probably with the code."

Li and Goldie went to the computer and connected the Friend-a-Wear with a cable. The code filled the screen. For the next few hours, they looked at the code line by line.

"It should work," Goldie said.

By dinnertime, the devices turned on and lit up, but not when they were supposed to.

"We're still missing something," Li said. They both knew who could help them, but neither said her name.

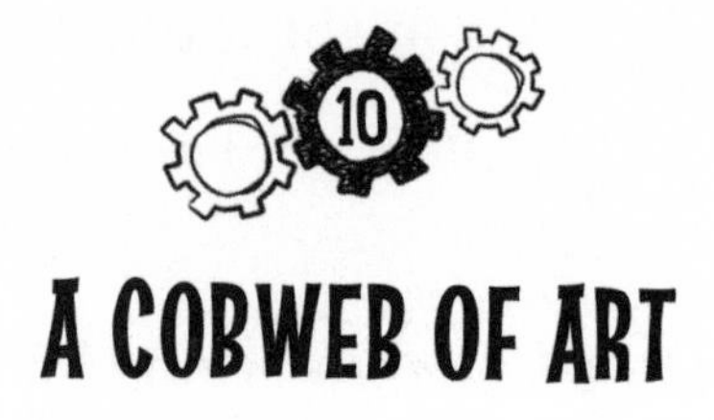

A COBWEB OF ART

For two days, Goldie sweated over Ruby's gift. She tweaked and made improvements. It definitely got better, but the Friend-a-Wear was still not right.

But now it was time to wrap the gift because the bash was today.

Goldie woke up early. Her bed's ejection mechanism tossed her across the room. She bounced off the trampoline, swung from the ceiling fan, flipped around the monkey bars, and landed perfectly in her fanciest overalls.

This was Ruby's big day, and Goldie was determined to make it special.

After a quick breakfast of spicy bacon waffles, she met Li in the driveway. He had all the birthday decorations packed into his bag.

"You ready, G?" Li asked as he strapped on his helmet.

Goldie put Ruby's present in her backpack and stepped on her skateboard. "Today is the day everything will be perfect for Ruby."

They raced through town to the smoothie shop. The party was only a few hours away, but Goldie could hardly wait. She wanted to see the surprised look on Ruby's face. But she really just wanted to see Ruby. She missed her BFF.

Miss Maggie met them at the door to Frothy Formulas.

"Hi, guys. Come on in." She waved. "I'm so

excited to host a party for Ruby."

"Thanks again, Miss Maggie," Goldie said.

They went inside. Goldie and Miss Maggie moved some tables to create a dance floor. Li set up an elaborate rope-ladder system in order to hang the streamers, signs, and balloons. It looked like a ropes course at an adventure park. He swung and jumped across the ceiling.

"I'm worried he'll fall," Miss Maggie said.

"We don't call him Li 'Gravity' Zhang for nothing," Goldie said. "He's part daredevil, part physicist."

Li's final touch was a giant disco ball that he quickly put together. Goldie flipped the light switch off. The smoothie shop sparkled with lights and color.

"It's perfect," Goldie said. They stood back and admired their work.

Val arrived a few minutes later. She

balanced the birthday cake in her arms. It was as big as a couch cushion.

"Wow, Val! You made that cake?" Goldie reached out to give her a hand.

"Yep. I spent all night—"

Crack! Pow!

A loud noise interrupted Val. The room shook.

"What was that?" Goldie asked.

But nobody had a chance to answer. A pipe broke through the wall. Water sprayed the room. Then the sprinklers in the ceiling all went off. There was a downpour in the smoothie shop.

"My cake!" Val screamed and ran outside.

Goldie dashed across the room and grabbed her gift. She tucked it in her hair. Then she joined Li, Miss Maggie, and Val in the parking lot.

"Miss M, I'm so, so sorry. It was all my fault." Li pulled off his wet hat. "I shouldn't have climbed your shop."

"No, dear, it's not your fault," Miss Maggie said. "Just a bit of bad luck. I'd better call the plumber." She pulled out her phone.

Li stood in front of the window. He watched his decorations get a not-needed shower. "Major bad luck," he said.

Goldie looked at the cake. Val had rescued it from the indoor rain. But she didn't think it mattered since they didn't have a place to hold the birthday bash.

"What do we do now?" Val asked Goldie.

Goldie looked at the water running out of Frothy Formulas. Even if they got the water turned off now, they couldn't get the place dry before the party. She peered at a clock inside the shop. They had less than an hour.

"We'll have the bash at the BloxShop," Goldie decided.

"Goldie," Val said, still holding the cake. "You know I love the BloxShop. We hang out there all the time. But it's a disaster. Like you put a junkyard and a tool shop in a blender, and then poured it out in a garage."

"It needs a little tidying, but I can engineer that." Goldie grabbed her skateboard.

"This I gotta see," Val said.

"Li, I need you to send a message to all the guests and let them know that the party is at a new address." Goldie pulled a guest list from her pocket. "I actually kept track of everyone who said they were coming, and I have their numbers."

Goldie was proud of herself. She was never this organized. All her teachers would say so. But this party was more important than homework. Of course, she wouldn't say that to her teachers or parents.

"And put a sign on the door." Goldie pointed to Frothy Formulas. "Just in case we miss someone."

"On it!" Li looked over the list.

"Miss Maggie, you'll still come to the party at the BloxShop, right?" Goldie asked.

She nodded and held up her phone. "As soon as the plumber is done."

Goldie grabbed her skateboard and pressed a button that doubled the length so two people could fit on it.

"Val, hop on. I'll give you a ride."

"No," Val said. "No, no, no. I'll drop the cake."

"We'll carry it together, and I promise to go slow." Goldie gave her friend a big toothy smile.

"But your idea of slow is faster than the speed of sound."

Goldie laughed. "I wish I could go faster than the speed of sound. We'll go Val-approved slow."

"Promise?" Val still sounded nervous.

"Promise."

Li hung a sign on the door. *Ruby's Birthday Bash Now at the BloxShop.* Goldie and Val climbed on the skateboard. They held the cake between them, which made steering difficult. But they did go slow. At one point on the ride home, they were passed by a crawling baby.

Goldie worried they wouldn't have time to set up.

When the BloxShop was in sight, Goldie whispered to Val, "Sorry." Then she pressed the turbo button on the skateboard, and they flew the last block.

“Gooooooldieeeeeeeeeeeeee!” Val screamed.

“It’s okay, Val. We’re here.” Goldie jumped off. The cake had survived the ride. Val had, too, but she was shaking quite a bit.

They went into the BloxShop. It did look like a blended mess. They set the cake on Goldie’s workbench.

Val grabbed a giant garbage bag. “Let’s get started,” she said.

“We’re going to need something bigger than that.” Goldie ran out of the shop and across to Li’s house. She rang the doorbell. Li’s grandpa answered.

“Hello, Goldie. Would you like to come in for some juice?” he asked.

Goldie shook her head. “No, thank you. May I borrow your riding lawn mower?”

“Sure. If it’s okay with your parents.” Mr. Zhang pointed to his shed.

Goldie nodded. She assumed it was okay with her parents. After all, she'd borrowed the lawn mower before.

In the shed, she found the lawn mower and several shovels. She tied the shovels to the front. Then she hopped in the driver's seat and rode to her yard. She located two more shovels and a rake and added them on, too.

"Yeehaw!" Goldie drove her cleanup plow

to the BloxShop. Once inside, she lowered the shovels. The plow pushed everything to the side.

“That’s one way to clean!” Val said, jumping out of the way.

Goldie cleared path after path until there was enough room to party. She parked the plow in the corner. She’d return it later. Now they needed to focus on decorations, and they only had ten minutes.

“Quick, Val. Find some string and paper or anything we can use to decorate.” Goldie dug through the pile of stuff she had created with the plow. She needed her T-shirt cannon. She’d seen one at a basketball game. The mascot loaded a T-shirt into the cannon, then pulled the trigger, sending the shirt into the crowd. Goldie had built her own. She used it to send her dirty laundry to the washing machine.

"Found it!" The T-shirt cannon was made from an old pipe, a bike pump, a garden hose, and other bits.

Val loaded it with string, paper, and glitter. Goldie drizzled in some glue so the decorations would stick.

"Hope this works," Val said.

Goldie pulled the paper-clip trigger. The string, bits of paper, and glitter flew onto the wall. It made a beautiful splatter design.

"I like it," Goldie said. They loaded the cannon again and again. They took aim at all the walls and the ceiling.

"Epic!" Li said when he arrived a few minutes later. "It's like a cobweb of art."

"Did you tell everyone about the change in

location?" Goldie asked.

"Yep." Li gave her a salute.

"Even Sarah Kumar and Zada?"

"Yep, even Sarah Kumar and Zada," he replied, just as there was a knock on the door. The guests were arriving.

"This is going to be a perfect bash," Goldie said. She pulled out her gift and placed it next to Val's cake. "I can't wait for Ruby."

"When will Ruby get here?" Val asked.

That's when Goldie realized she'd forgotten one detail.

Ruby!

TIE THEM UP

"I forgot about Ruby!" Goldie exclaimed. "I mean, I didn't forget about her." She motioned to the party in the BloxShop. "This is all for her. But I forgot we need to get her here. That should have been step one: how to get the guest of honor to the top-secret party without ruining the surprise."

"I guess we started at step two," Li said.

"We all forgot," Val said.

More and more guests filed in. Li turned on

music. Nacho carried around a bowl of punch on his head.

"What are we going to do, G?" Li asked.

"Don't worry. I can engineer this." Goldie started to pace. "We could build an army of mini-robots and send them across Bloxtown to find Ruby."

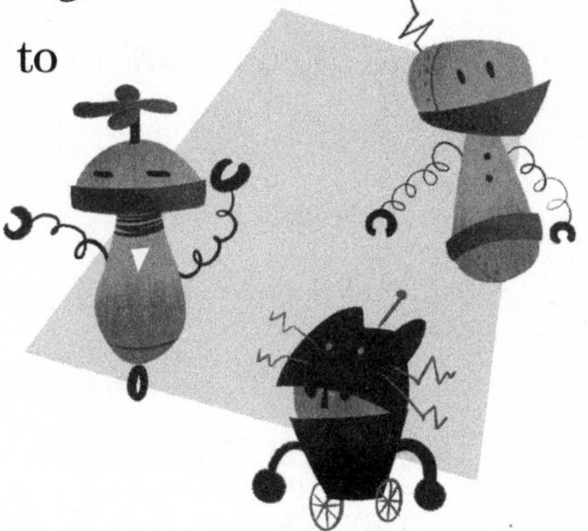

"Or we could—" Val started, but Goldie cut her off.

"But we probably don't have enough batteries to power all those mini-robots." Goldie scratched her head. "Or we could hack into a government satellite and redirect it to find Ruby."

Val tried to share her idea again. "Or we could—"

"But we need Ruby's help to hack into anything. She's the expert hacker." Goldie tapped a finger to her chin. "We could use a plane to skywrite an invitation. It would have to be big enough that all of Bloxtown could see it."

"Or we could—"

"But then we'd need a pilot—"

"Goldie!" Now it was Val's turn to interrupt. "Just try calling her." Val shoved a phone into Goldie's hand.

"That might work." Goldie put the phone to her ear. It rang and rang. But no one answered.

"Leave a message," Val said.

Goldie nodded. "Hey, Rubes. It's Goldie. Just leaving you a message. Does anyone leave messages anymore? Nothing's going on. But I thought you might want to come over to the BloxShop today. Like soon. Maybe even right now. No biggie. Just miss you. Okay. Bye. Come over now!"

Val stared at Goldie with wide eyes. "That wasn't weird at all."

"We need to find her!" Goldie clenched her hands into fists. She'd find Ruby if she had to search every last corner of Bloxtown. She'd look under every rock, behind every tree, and in every trash can. Though she knew Ruby would never be in a trash can.

But she couldn't even walk across her BloxShop because it was crowded with guests. Including two VIPs.

Sarah Kumar, the coder extraordinaire, came over to Goldie. "Great party," she said. "But I can't stay long. I have a deadline. When can I meet Ruby Rails?"

"Soon," Goldie said. "Any minute." *Hopefully.*

Val stepped in. "In the meantime, have you had any punch?" She escorted Sarah Kumar to Nacho for a drink.

Goldie needed a solution, and quick. No robots. No hacking. No skywriting. And calling hadn't worked.

Someone tapped her on the shoulder. She turned to see Zada.

"Goldie, darling. Thank you for inviting me. This is quite a fun party. I've met the most wonderful people, but I still haven't met Ruby. Where is the birthday girl?"

"Um . . . somewhere." Goldie peeked into the crowd, hoping that Ruby might magically appear.

"I'd really like to meet her, but then I must be gone. My plane is waiting. I'm off to Paris this evening." Zada adjusted her handbag on her shoulder. She seemed ready to leave.

"Okay," Goldie said. "Let me go find Ruby. Just hang out for a few minutes. Have you met my dog? He loves your fashion designs. He chews them all up."

Goldie pushed through the guests. She hoped Zada assumed that Ruby was just among the crowd.

"Li!" she called. "Val!"

Her friends came running.

"We need to split up and find Ruby," Goldie said. She handed them each a walkie-talkie.

"What about the party and the guests?" Val asked.

"Yeah," Li agreed. "If we leave, everyone might leave, G."

"Okay. Val, you stay here and make sure no one leaves. Especially Sarah Kumar and Zada. Do whatever it takes. Lock the doors."

"That's probably against fire code," Val said.

"Tie them up," Goldie suggested.

"That's probably against the law," Val said.

"Just make sure they stay." Goldie turned to Li. "You search the part of town north of the park. I'll do the south half."

"We'll find her, G," Li said.

"And I'll keep the guests here," Val added.

Goldie nodded. This had to work. She couldn't risk a best friend fail again. Ruby might not have known about the party, but she might think Goldie had forgotten her birthday. Goldie wouldn't let that happen.

FRIEND-A-WEAR

Goldie rode her skateboard to the park. The entire way she called Ruby's name.

"Did you lose your dog, dear?" asked a woman pushing a stroller.

"Ruby isn't my dog," Goldie explained. "She's one of my best friends. She's a Gearhead."

There was no sign of Ruby at the park. Goldie used her walkie-talkie to call Li and Val.

"How's it going? Any sign of Ruby?" she asked.

"Negative," Li answered. "I've covered seven blocks. I haven't seen her."

"Val?"

"She's not here. And the guests are getting restless. They're playing charades now, but I don't know how long I can hold them," Val said.

Goldie needed to move fast. She flew down the streets and stopped at all of Ruby's favorite places—the library, the computer store, the designer sock shop. She asked everyone, "Have you seen Ruby?" and the answer was always no.

The walkie-talkie crackled. Li's voice came through. Goldie felt a surge of hope.

"Tried Ruby's house. No one is home."

"Keep looking," Goldie said.

"Um . . . we have a problem," Val said. "Zada left."

"No!" Goldie cried.

"Sorry. I tried everything to get her to stay," Val explained. "I wrapped myself around one of her legs and Nacho grabbed the other, but she still escaped. I did manage to keep one of her shoes, though."

"Is Sarah Kumar still there?" Goldie asked.

"For now," Val answered.

"Don't let her leave." Goldie got off the walkie-talkie. She rode to Frothy Formulas, the museum, and the little shops on Main Street. She showed everyone Ruby's picture. No one had seen her.

Goldie started to think the surprise party had been a mistake. She'd spent a week planning and setting everything up. And during that week she'd hardly spoken to Ruby. She didn't know what her friend had been up to or what she had planned. Goldie had pushed Ruby aside to make room for her BFF's birthday bash.

"Goldie," Val said through the walkie-talkie. "Sarah Kumar is leaving. I can't stop her! What should I do?"

"Nothing," Goldie said quietly. "Let her go."

"Really?" both Li and Val asked at the same time.

"I can't show Ruby how much she means to me in one day when I haven't had time for her all week." Goldie got off her skateboard and sat on the curb.

"Do you want me to keep looking?" Li asked.

"No. We'll see her tomorrow at school. And I'll talk to her then." Goldie knew what she had to say. She had to apologize for messing up HackerCon and for not spending any time with her lately. And for missing her birthday.

"Should I tell everyone else to go home?" Val asked.

"Yeah. I'll be back in a little while." She turned off the walkie-talkie.

Goldie tucked her skateboard under her arm and started home. She wasn't in the mood to ride. The walk took almost an hour, and she noticed a lot more than she did when she flew by on her board. She marveled at a bird's nest in a tree. That nest had been built using found materials. Birds were brilliant engineers.

By the time she got to the BloxShop, she felt a little better. She didn't always need to go through life at top speed. Sometimes it was good to slow down.

Goldie opened the door. Val, Li, and Nacho were taking down the decorations.

"Thanks for your help, Gearheads. I couldn't have done any of this without you." It still felt weird to say *Gearheads* without Ruby being there.

They cleaned the BloxShop together.

"What should we do with the cake?" Val asked. "I feel bad cutting it without Ruby."

A voice came from the doorway.

"Luckily, you don't have to." It was Ruby!

Li, Val, and Goldie ran to her. They swarmed her in a group hug. Nacho nudged his way in.

"What are you doing here? Where have you

been? Are you okay? Are you having a good birthday?" Goldie asked every question in her brain.

Ruby nodded when they released her from the huddle.

"My family and I went to the beach for the day," she explained. "When we got back, I heard your message and came right over."

"I'm so glad you did." Goldie hugged her again. "We planned a perfect birthday bash for you."

"Except we forgot one detail," Val said. "You."

Ruby laughed.

"We even invited your favorite people," Goldie continued. "Sarah Kumar and Zada."

"Sarah? And Zada? You invited them? And they were *here*?" Ruby's eyes were huge with excitement.

"Yes. But they left because I messed up. Again. I had too much going on. I'm sorry, Ruby. I blew it."

"You didn't blow it." Ruby grabbed her hand. "It just didn't work out. Besides, they aren't my favorite people."

"They're not?" Val asked. She squished her eyebrows together.

"Nope. My favorite people are right here." She pointed to Li, then to Val, and finally to Goldie. "I've missed you."

"We've missed you, too," Val said.

"Ditto," Li said.

"I can't believe you did all this for me. And you're wearing your best overalls," Ruby said. "I thought . . . Never mind."

"What did you think?" Goldie asked.

"I thought you didn't want to be my friend. I thought you didn't have time for me." Ruby crossed her arms.

"I *didn't* have time," Goldie admitted. "But I've always wanted to be your friend, and I always will be. I'd do anything for my Gearheads."

"Me too," Val said. "I climbed the side of a building for you."

Ruby laughed when they told her the story of breaking into Sarah Kumar's building.

"I wish I had been there," Ruby said.

"Let's do it again," Li suggested.

"No!" Val yelled. "Can we just eat cake?"

They sang "Happy Birthday" and then cut the cake. Ruby, Val, and Li thought it was delicious. Goldie sprinkled a few bacon bits on top. It was the best cake she'd ever had.

"I have a present for you," Goldie said. "But it doesn't work quite right." She handed Ruby the wrapped box.

Ruby carefully opened the gift. She pulled out four matching bracelets. Along the band was a black charm in the shape of a gear.

"I call it the Friend-a-Wear," Goldie said. She handed one to each of the Gearheads. "It's supposed to light up and smell nice when I'm thinking about you."

Goldie pressed the gear on her bracelet. The gear on Ruby's turned pink for a second but then faded.

"It still has some bugs in the code."

Ruby looked at her bracelet. "I think I can fix this." She borrowed a cable and connected her bracelet to her minicomputer. Then she examined the code. "Aha!" she said. She typed on the keyboard for a few seconds.

Goldie, Li, and Val watched.

"Try it now," Ruby said as she pulled off the cable.

Goldie pressed the button again. Ruby's bracelet glowed pink, and she sniffed. "I smell flowers."

"It works!" Goldie pumped her fist in the air. They tried each of their bracelets. They glowed different colors and had different scents. Goldie's smelled of maple syrup. Val had vanilla. Li had orange.

"Now we'll always know when we're thinking of each other," Ruby said.

"Yep, but it's not really necessary," Goldie said. "Because I'm always thinking about my Gearheads."

"Even when making waffles?" Val asked.

"Yep."

"Even when designing rockets?" Ruby asked.

"Absolutely."

"Even when time traveling?" Li asked.

"Yes. At least, I think so. If I travel back a hundred years, can I think about Gearheads before we even existed?" Goldie grabbed a wrench. "I guess we'll have to find out."

GoldieBlox is the award-winning children's multimedia company disrupting the pink aisle in toy stores globally and challenging gender stereotypes with the world's first girl engineer character. Through the integration of storytelling and STEM (Science, Technology, Engineering, and Math) principles, GoldieBlox creates toys, books, apps, videos, animation, and merchandise; the tools that empower girls to build their confidence, dreams, and, ultimately, their futures.

GoldieBlox was created by Debbie Sterling.

Learn more and shop at GoldieBlox.com.

Follow us on social media at @goldieblox.